Stranded With A Ravenous Shifter

Marooned For A Night

Olivia T. Turner

www.OliviaTTurner.com

Edited by Karen Collins Editing

To Steve,
Who really knew how to spend a weekend in a cabin.

Chapter One

Tara

"Oh, my god," my sister Cynthia says as she walks into the room with her hand over her mouth and a tear in her eye. "You look stunning."

I yank up my wedding dress, sprint across the room, and slam the door closed.

She jerks her head back in surprise as I grab two fistfuls of her bridesmaid dress and yank her to an inch from my face. "You have to get me out of here!" I screech. I can hear the panic in my voice. My eyes are wild and unblinking. My heart is pounding so hard it's vibrating through my chest. I need to get the fuck out of here. Now!

"Whoa whoa whoa," she says softly as she puts a gentle hand on my shoulder, trying to calm me down. My grip tightens so hard my knuckles are burning. "You have to breathe, Tara. You're just nervous."

She doesn't understand. I *can't* do this. I *won't* do this.

This wedding is *not* happening.

"Just let me go," she says with a hint of worry in her voice. "You're going to tear my dress."

She tries to gently ease my hands off of her, but they're clenched on tight.

"Let go, Tara!" she says as she tries harder to pry my fingers off. "What are you doing?!"

I let go of her and start pacing around the room like a wild tiger trapped in a small cage. My whole body is as tight as a bowstring, my adrenaline is surging, sweat is pouring down my back. I'm ready to snap.

My sister looks at the closed door as I pace around the room, probably wondering if she can unload her maid of honor duties onto some poor unsuspecting cousin out there.

"These are just wedding day jitters," she says in a soothing voice. "Perfectly normal."

"This is not *normal!*" I screech as I grab a handful of hair and yank it out of my perfectly coiffed hairdo. She winces as threads of auburn hair come tumbling down.

I'm pretty sure that normal jitters don't make you feel like the whole world is ending. Like there's a black hole beside you and you're desperately trying to stop your soul from getting sucked into it.

"You need to chill," she says in her big-sister-get-your-head-out-of-your-ass voice. "You're supposed to be walking down the aisle in like five minutes."

"I told you, I'm not doing that!"

"You agreed to it!"

"I don't care!" I shout as I cover my eyes with my hands.

"David is standing at the aisle waiting for you. You're going to stand him up?"

"Yes!" I shout as I throw my hands in the air. "That's *exactly* what I'm going to do!"

Cynthia takes a step back. She's watching me like you'd watch an unhinged lunatic that you're stuck in an elevator with.

I can't blame her for that. My jaw is clenched, I have crazy eyes, I'm sweating, and my hair is coming undone. She's probably wondering why I suddenly turned feral.

"I'm sorry that David is going to be upset," I say. "Truly, I am. But I barely know the guy!"

"I thought the dates with him went well."

"Dates?" I say with a deranged chuckle. "Those weren't dates."

Cynthia doesn't know what to do. She keeps looking at the door.

"I better get Mom."

"No!" I shout as I lunge forward and grab her arm so hard she screams. "You can't!"

Mom is the one who set this all up. If she comes in here, I'll never be able to escape.

I'm twenty-four-years-old and have never even had a boyfriend. Rent and house prices are insane right now and of course, I can't afford either of them, so I've been stuck living at home with my parents. My mother has been trying to marry me off for years now, and I finally cracked.

My parents want to sell their home and downsize in Buenos Aires, Argentina for their retirement. Mom spent a year abroad there when she was young and always dreamed of moving back one day. She finally got Dad on board, so the only thing left to do was unload me onto some poor unsuspecting schmuck.

That's where my groom David came in. My mother him up for *months*. Every day, all I heard was David David that.

7

'David has a new car, Tara. It's blue. Isn't your favorite color blue?'

'David has the nicest eyes. Wouldn't you like your children to have nice eyes?'

'Did you know that David got promoted at work? He's an assistant manager now. Sounds like marriage material to me.'

She would go on and on and on and fucking on about arranged marriages too.

While I was eating breakfast - 'That's how most of the world picks their spouses, Tara, did you know that?'

While I was trying to read - 'Divorce rates are lower for arranged marriages, Tara, did you know that?'

While doing my laundry - 'Couples with arranged marriages are happier, Tara, did you know that?'

While trying to sleep - 'You're more likely to win the lottery if you have an arranged marriage, Tara, did you know that?'

I must have been worn down and sleep-deprived from all of the nagging, because I finally threw my hands in the air and shouted, 'Fine! I'll marry David just leave me alone!'

She wasted no time in setting it up. She wasn't about to give me a second to regroup, recharge, and realize that this was a horrible idea. David was at my house (with his parents) for dinner three days later.

It was strange to say the least. It felt like we were the main exhibit in a freak museum with all four of our parents watching us like hawks all night. Every time we tried to talk, they would stop their conversation and lean in to listen, so we barely said a word.

The next week, my parents and I were at their house. We had some alone time while we set the table. We talked about five things:

1. Pretzels (he likes them but prefers chips)

2. The napkins on the table which belonged to his grandmother (they were painfully ugly)

3. The weather (it was cloudy)

4. The dinner (should be ready soon)

5. His fantasy football team (I don't or won't ever give a shit about fantasy football)

There was zero chemistry. Zero fireworks. Zero interest.

Looking at him made me feel as much passion as looking at a stalk of celery lying on the dirty tiled floor of the grocery store.

But things were in motion—our mothers working quickly behind the scenes—and all of a sudden we had a wedding date and my mother came home with a dress and the invitations were sent out before I even knew they were ordered.

And now I'm stuck in the backroom of the church with my sister, trying to fight back a panic attack.

"I can't marry him, Cynthia," I say as my hands start shaking. "Mom said he had beautiful eyes. They're not even that nice!"

"There's more to him than just his eyes."

"There was no spark," I say, feeling the panic bubbling back up. "I need some kind of spark at least. Is that too much to ask? You know me, Cyn. I cry at love songs. I watched The Notebook at least a hundred times. I want a passionate love affair. I want a man who will sweep me off my feet! I want to be around someone I'm so into that it's a struggle not to rip their clothes off whenever I look at them. I don't want boring David and his stupid fantasy football team!"

"Hate to break it to you, Tara, but every guy out there has a fantasy football team. It's an epidemic."

"I can't marry him!" I screech. "I know I said I would, but I can't."

"Let's just breathe slowly," Cynthia says as she walks to the door and grabs the handle. "We'll walk over to the aisle and when you see your handsome groom standing at the alter, I'm sure you'll change your mind."

"I won't."

"Let's try."

My eyes narrow on her. "You're my maid of honor, Cynthia. Do your job."

"I'm trying to," she says, huffing out in exasperation. "I'm trying to calm you down."

"You shouldn't be trying to calm me down!" I say with my voice rising. "You should be getting me car keys and distracting everyone while I climb out the window and make a run for it."

Her shoulders drop and she looks at me. For the first time today, she's really looking at me.

"You really don't want to do this?"

I shake my head.

"Alright." She bursts into action. The panic in me starts to subside now that she's on my team.

"Take my car," she says as she grabs her purse and pulls out her keys. "You'll need this too." She gives me all the cash she has on her and I shove it into my bra. "I have clothes in my trunk that you can change into."

"Thank you!" I say as I grab her hand and cling to it. "I'll never forget this!"

"Where are you going to go?"

"I don't know," I say as my mind races. I never thought past getting out of this room.

"Go to those cabins in Montana that we used to stay at," she says. "In Caldwell. Remember those?"

"Yes! That's perfect."

"They're about two hours away," she says as she hurries me over to the window. "Lay low there for a couple of days until Mom cools down."

"I don't have my phone!"

"It's okay," she says as she gives me her credit card. "For emergencies only! I'll call the main desk and ask for you when everything has calmed down."

"You don't mind breaking the news to everyone?" I say as she opens the stained glass window. Cold winter air hits us like a slap in the face.

"Do I mind going into that full church and announcing to everyone that you left?" she says with a laugh. "What do you think?"

"Thank you!" I kiss her cheek and she boosts me up. I climb through the window and stop before leaping out. "You're the best sister ever."

She shakes her head, but there's a smile on her face. "And you're the craziest sister ever."

I blow her a kiss and then leap down. My beautiful satin slingback pointed-toe pumps land in cold wet slush.

Frigid January wind slams into my bare arms as I hit the unlock button on Cynthia's key.

Her little mint green car lights up and I grin when I spot it.

A few minutes later, I'm blasting the heat, blasting the radio, and singing at the top of my lungs while I barrel down the highway—the church nothing more than a speck in my rearview mirror.

Chapter Two

Leo

"Get this," my older brother Michael says as I grab my ax and bring it crashing down onto a log. It explodes apart. "Leo doesn't think he needs a mate."

My younger brother Oliver bursts out laughing. He drops the tree he's dragging through the snow and doubles over, holding his ribs.

I roll my eyes as I pick up another log and place it on the chopping block. These two guys are so fucking frustrating.

"Tell me why I built my cabin so close to you pricks?" I ask as I squeeze the ax and then heave it over my head. I exhale hard as I bring it down. It slams into the thick piece of oak with a *thunk* and slices right through it.

"Because you love us," Michael says with a laugh as he rips the branches off a fallen tree trunk with his bare hands.

"And because you're too cheap to buy your own land,"

Oliver says as he picks up the tree, hoists it onto his shoulder, and comes walking over, trudging through the thick snow.

I'm not too cheap. It's because this land is perfect. Our parents left us sixty-eight acres of pristine mountain wilderness in Montana. I'd be crazy to turn that down. My grizzly bear loves it. He would be devastated if we moved.

Once we inherited the land, the three Brook brothers each built a cabin tucked away in a little private section of the forest. I can't see either of my brothers' cabins from my porch, but I still see them constantly. This mountain is feeling smaller and smaller every day.

"But seriously," Oliver says as he drops the tree at Michael's feet. Oliver is dragging the trees over, Michael is stripping the branches, and I'm chopping them up. We can feel a big snowstorm coming on and we're stocking up on firewood in case we lose electricity for a few days. "You really don't think you need a mate?"

I shrug. "I think I'll be fine without one."

Michael and Oliver smirk at each other.

"It's true," I say. "I'm twenty-eight. I've been fine until now."

"And what does your bear have to say about it?" Oliver asks with a grin.

I huff out a breath as I line up another log on the chopping block. My inner grizzly bear has been fine all this time, but I can tell he wants to find our mate. I do too, more than anything, but all of this waiting and worrying and wondering and constant obsessing over this fantasy girl who may not ever come is starting to get to me. I feel like my life has been on pause mode for the past few years while I wait for her to show up.

I want to get on with it already. I want to live my life, even if she's not in it.

I just want more than this purgatory I've been living in. I want to move forward.

My brothers don't understand. They're more than happy to wait one hundred lifetimes for their mates to show up.

"My bear does what *I* tell it," I say as I split another log in two. "*I'm* the one who makes the rules. *I'm* the one in charge."

Michael rolls his eyes as he rips off a thick branch. "Wait until your mate shows up. Then, you'll find out you ain't in charge of shit."

"Yeah," Oliver says as he heads back to grab another fallen tree. "I'm with Mikey on this one. Giving up waiting for your mate... That's sacrilege. Being on the lookout for our mates, waiting, saving ourselves, holding our breath—it's all part of it, man. It's just going to make it that much sweeter when she arrives."

"Yeah, well I'm done waiting," I say as I shove the ax into the chopping block so hard half the blade disappears. "And I'm done with this."

Michael and Oliver watch me as I storm off into the thick snow.

"We're not done here!" Michael shouts as I head for the forest. "The storm will be here in an hour!"

I don't turn around. I just trudge forward as my inner grizzly paces around.

"I guess we're chopping the rest of the wood ourselves," Oliver mumbles behind me.

I don't even care. I'm too frustrated. I'm too amped up.

I talk a big game, saying that I don't need my mate, but I know as well as my brothers do that it's all bullshit.

15

I need her badly.

I'm just so sick of feeling so helpless. I'm tired of waiting for this amazing future that I know is ahead of me and not being able to do anything to make it arrive faster.

It's torture.

My bear grumbles inside me as I walk under the large canopy of trees. It's about dinner time and it's already getting dark. The snowstorm is coming in faster than we'd expected, but I can't exactly go lock myself in my cabin when I'm feeling like this. I'll go crazy in there. I'll tear the place apart.

"Come on," I whisper to my bear as I pull off my shirt and hang it on a tree. The cold wind whips my bare skin as I pull off my boots, and then my jeans and underwear. I tuck them into the nook of a thick branch where they hopefully won't get covered in snow and I'll have to wait until spring to find them.

My inner grizzly is hovering near the surface, ready to come out.

I need a break from my life right now. I need a break from this reality where my mate is not with me.

So, I set my grizzly free.

He bursts out of me as I'm pulled inside.

Suddenly, I'm seeing the world through his eyes. I'm experiencing it through his senses—the smell of pine, of the approaching storm, the scent of a fox who passed by earlier this morning. The cool tingling of the wind on his fur, the feel of his paws in the cold snow, the taste of water in the air, which always comes before an intense snowstorm.

I sigh as I sink into the darkness and let him take over.

Where is she?

Where is my mate? I'm twenty-eight years old.

Shouldn't she be here by now? What the hell is fate waiting for?

As my bear wanders through the woods, I wonder if the fault is mine.

I mean, how am I going to find my mate if I spend most of my time hiding out in the woods with my two single brothers? It's not like we run into a ton of women up here. Or any. Maybe I should get out more.

Maybe I should start being more proactive.

I sigh as my grizzly stops to smell a bush where a rabbit wandered by earlier.

Or, maybe I should just give up for real.

Maybe my brothers are wrong.

Do I even really need a mate?

Chapter Three

Tara

All I see is white.

The windshield wipers on my sister's crappy old car get an A for effort, but they're not doing much in this hellish snowstorm. They're screeching in pain as they whip from side to side, pushing away the endless snow that keeps coming and coming and coming. Even when they clear the glass for a split second, a blanket of fresh snow is there to immediately replace it. I can't see anything.

My hands are gripping the steering wheel so tight they're hurting, but I still can't seem to loosen my grip.

I'm on the highway somewhere in Montana. It's dark out and there are only a few other cars on the snow-covered road—people with death wishes, people who don't believe in checking the emergency weather reports, and one runway bride who is in way over her head.

"What do I do? What do I do?" I mutter as I press down on the gas with my heart pounding. The worst part is, there's so much snow on the road that I have to go fast. If I slow down, I'll get stuck and then some pickup truck or a snowplow is going to ram into me from behind.

But the faster I go, the more I slip and slide. I keep losing control. It's terrifying.

I can't pull over. I can't do anything.

"*Forty-one inches of snow,*" the male announcer on the radio says with a laugh. "*This is shaping up to be one heck of a storm.*"

"*I hope none of our listeners are on the road now,*" the female announcer says.

"*Surely our listeners aren't stupid enough for that,*" the male announcer says with a laugh. I want to smack him. "*After all the warnings we've been giving to stay in your homes.*"

I smack the radio off instead.

Forty-one inches is *a lot* of snow. I'm suddenly realizing how dangerous this situation is. My sister's car has the power of a lawnmower and I doubt she's changed the tires in the past decade. I'm wearing nothing but my pointed-toe pumps that only cover half my foot and there's no winter jacket in here, no boots, no woollen hat, no big fluffy mittens.

If I slide off the road, I'm going to be covered in snow within minutes. They'll thaw me out in spring. I'll be a global news story. An Internet sensation. I can see the headline now—*Runaway Bride's Cold Feet Leads to Frozen Fate.*

My tires hit something slippery and I let out a shrill scream as my car starts spinning wildly. Control is lost. The steering wheel does nothing.

"SHIT!!!" I scream as the spinning accelerates, launching me in tight circles down the snowy highway.

What are you supposed to do in this situation again? Steer into the turn? Steer away from the turn? Brake? Accelerate?

Instead of trying any of those options, I just scream as loud as I can and slam my feet on both pedals to hedge my bets.

Shockingly, it doesn't work. My car flies off the road and crashes *hard* into a pile of packed snow.

The windshield shatters into spiderwebs, the metal frame crunches, my head flies forward, and the top of my nose slams into the steering wheel so hard that a jolt of pain shoots through my brain.

"*Oh... fuck...*" I moan as I drop the back of my head onto the seat. Warm liquid starts leaking down my face. My eyes are watering, but I can tell that the warm liquid is not my tears.

"*Shit...*" I whisper as I turn the rearview mirror and look at myself. There's a nasty gash on the bridge of my nose with blood pouring down all over my face and chest. I taste metal.

But as bad as my nose is, it's not my biggest problem. The cold is already coming in, leaking through the cracks in the windows and snaking along my skin like a frigid ghost. Goosebumps rise on my flesh. I shiver. Once, twice, then non-stop.

It's freezing in here.

I shake the daze out of my head and look around. All of the windows are broken except for one in the back.

The snow keeps coming down and by the time I can get my seatbelt off, it's covering every window. I'm drowning in it.

"You can't stay here."

The voice just comes out of me. Staying here will mean certain death.

I'll freeze to death, I'll bleed to death, I'll starve to death —pick your poison. If I get out, I'll have a chance. A small chance, but a chance.

"Get the clothes in the trunk," I whisper to myself. "Then try to flag someone down on the highway."

I take a deep breath, pop the trunk, and then try to push the door open. The snow stops it from opening more than a foot, so I kick the broken window out and then climb through that.

Frigid wind and whipping snow slam into me as I step onto the snow. My leg sinks into it up to my waist. I'm chilled to the bone. My skeleton feels like it's covered in ice. I pull my leg up to take another step and my shoe is gone.

"Keep going," I tell myself as I work my way to the trunk, leaving a trail of red behind me. Snow pours down— covering my head, filling the trunk, and hiding my car.

The highway is empty. My car is so far from it that all the energy leaves my body when I see how far I have to walk through the high snow to get back to it.

"Ignore it," I whisper through chattering teeth as I push my way to the trunk. One step at a time.

I grab Cynthia's clothes and try putting them on, but I'm so cold that my fingers are becoming numb. Buttons and zippers are out of the question. It's hard to maneuver my hands, so I just start wrapping articles of clothing around me the best I can.

Bright spotlights light up the road. I gasp as I turn around and see a line of two snowplows coming toward me.

"Over here!" I scream with the last of my energy as I wave my arms. "Over here!"

No...

They drive right past me. They don't even slow down.

That was the last of my hope.

I feel it shrinking inside me as I watch them disappear into the distance.

I'm alone again. In the dark snowy mountains.

A low rumbling growl vibrates behind me.

I'm not alone.

I wish I was alone.

My stomach drops as I slowly turn around and see a gigantic grizzly bear with his eyes locked on me. He comes stalking out of the forest with his head hung low.

I swallow hard as I stare at him in horror.

White snow clings to his brown fur as he approaches with his intense eyes *fixated* on me. His mouth drops open and he lets out an angry huff. His teeth are so long. So sharp. So white.

I can't stop staring at them as he makes his way over, those huge shoulders moving like boulders with every step.

Would I rather freeze to death or get eaten to death?

The question hovers in my mind for a second, but I already know the answer. I'd rather be a human popsicle than have those sharp teeth skewering my body and tearing me to pieces.

I leap into the trunk with the last bit of energy I can muster as the huge grizzly rushes forward.

"No!" I scream as I grab the trunk and yank it down, clicking it into place.

I'm plunged into darkness as the vicious bear roars in fury.

That was close...

I can hear my heart pounding through my body as I wait in silence. I'm really fucked now. I'm stuck in this trunk with no heating and even if there wasn't a hungry grizzly bear waiting for me outside, I still wouldn't be able to open it.

My car is going to be covered in snow any minute, which will make finding me impossible, even if someone was trying to look, which no one is.

I should have just married David.

But even as I think it, I know it's not true. That would have been a slow death over decades, and nothing is worse than that.

At least, I'm going out on my own terms. Kind of.

The trunk suddenly clicks and springs open.

"What the hell?!" I screech as I lunge up to quickly close it. Since when do grizzly bears know how to operate trunks?!?

I grab it, pull it down, but a big strong hand darts out and stops me halfway. He yanks the trunk back open, bringing me up with it.

My mouth drops as a man steps into view. A *naked* man.

His brown eyes are staring at me in awe. I'm staring back at him in awe too, but mostly because he's out here in this horrible storm naked and doesn't seem to be bothered in the least.

"I'm going to get you out of here," he says in a calm voice full of authority.

I just stare up at him, completely mesmerized. "Okay."

He slides his big muscular arms under me and picks me up easily.

I'm expecting him to be as cold as I am, but his skin is so warm. It's like cuddling up to a heater. He holds me to his muscular chest and I press my face against it, stealing as much of that warmth radiating off him as I can.

He carries me to the passenger side of the car and yanks the door open.

"Stay in here," he says as he carefully lowers me onto the seat. I immediately feel the cold again as he pulls his warm arms away. "I'll pull the car onto the road."

'How the heck are you going to do that?' I'm about to ask, but I go speechless when I turn and see his giant naked cock hanging *low* between his muscular legs. It's right in front of my face.

It's all I can think about as he slams the door closed and I'm alone in the car once again.

It wasn't that big, was it?! I keep asking myself

I get jerked forward as the car starts moving backward.

"What is happening?!" I whisper as I turn and watch this man pulling my sister's car through several feet of snow. He drags it all the way back to the highway and then gets in behind the wheel.

I just stare at him with my mouth hanging open as he tries to start the engine. He turns the key and pumps the gas with his foot until it roars back to life.

"*Yes,*" he says as he smacks the steering wheel in celebration.

I can't celebrate. I'm too confused. Why was this man able to pull a car through that thick snow? Why is he naked? Where did he come from? Oh yeah, and where the fuck did that bear go?

I can't understand any of this. I must have gotten a brain injury from the crash. Or, maybe the paramedics found me and I'm on some wild painkillers. Am I hallucinating all of this?

If this is a hallucination, then he surely won't mind me gawking at him.

I run my eyes up and down this man's naked body as I

tremble on the seat. His legs are like muscular tree trunks. His arms deserve their own fan club. His face... God, his face. He's beautiful. His chest... has my blood smeared all over it.

I swallow hard as I take another look at his long thick cock. My breath hitches as I stare at his thick shaft and masculine balls. It's the first one I've seen in person, and it's surpassing *all* expectations.

He turns to me. I dart my guilty eyes up to his.

"You look freezing," he whispers as he jacks up the heat. "Come sit on my lap."

He reaches for me and I fight back a gulp.

"Okay."

It's all I can say as he grabs me with those forceful hands and pulls me onto his muscular thighs. My ass slides across his thick cock and I feel it getting harder under me.

Those warm comforting arms squeeze me tightly as he starts driving down the highway at a reckless speed.

"Give me your feet," he commands.

"My f-feet?"

He reaches down, grabs them, and swallows all ten of my toes in his big warm hand. It slowly brings life back into them.

I'm worried we're going to end up on the side of the road again, maybe upside down this time, but he's an excellent driver and we stay in the middle of the lane.

His warmth engulfs me as the wind and snow whip in through the window I kicked out. I bury my face into his warm chest and focus on the beating of his heart as he takes me... I don't know where he's taking me...

"I have to get to Caldwell," I tell him in a shaky voice thanks to my chattering teeth.

"That's over one hundred miles away," he says in a deep

voice that rumbles through me. "I'm bringing you to my cabin."

Normally, I'd be fighting with a naked stranger who was trying to force me into his weird little secluded cabin in the mountains, but I just stare at his Adam's apple and nod. "Okay."

I guess I'm heading to this naked guy's cabin...

In the mountains...

Where no one will ever find me...

Not worrisome at all.

Chapter Four

Leo

I'm clinging onto my girl as I drive this shit car down the icy highway as fast as I can. The tires are practically bald, and the protective side of me wants to give her a lecture on road safety, but she's in no condition for that.

The poor girl keeps shaking. She's trembling non-stop with purple lips. But it's that nasty gash on her nose that I'm really worried about.

I keep looking down at it as I cradle her to my chest, hoping the warmth of my naked body is enough to keep her from entering hypothermic shock.

"We're almost there," I whisper to her as I yank the car off the highway and head onto the road that leads to my property. There's so much snow. The car is barely making it through. It's groaning and squealing as I push it beyond what it was designed for.

Come on, I say, willing the engine to make it.

My cabin is in view when it finally dies. The engine just gives out with a pathetic sputter, and the heater turns off. The dashboard goes dark.

"What happened?" my girl asks as those stunning green eyes dart up to mine. She's so breathtaking. Even with her face covered in blood, she's the most beautiful thing I've ever seen.

There's no doubt in my mind that she's my mate. No doubt at all.

My grizzly smelled her on the cold wind and we both knew immediately. It was like a shock to the system. Her scent burned like fire as it blazed down our throat.

"The car died," I whisper as I hold her a little tighter. "But my cabin is just up ahead. I'll carry you to it."

"Okay."

I slide my arm under her legs and around her back. I kick the door open and then carry her, running toward my cabin through the thick snow.

Even though I'm naked, the cold doesn't bother me. But I know it's different for her. She's already been out here for way too long. I have to get her warmed up inside before frostbite begins claiming parts of this stunning body that I'm already becoming obsessed with.

Why is she wearing a wedding dress?

That question keeps nibbling at the back of my mind, but I push it out every time it rears its ugly face. I can't focus on that right now. I need to get her to safety first.

She's clinging to me as I open the front door and bring her inside.

Her teeth are still chattering as I look around. The fireplace is cold. The bath is going to take too long to fill. She needs warmth and I'm the best option to give it to her.

I bring her to my bedroom and lay her on the bed.

"I'll be right back," I say as I run to the bathroom, dump some bubble bath into the tub, and turn it on.

Before the water even hits the ceramic, I'm back in my room, going to her.

She looks shell-shocked as she sits on the bed, watching me with stunned eyes. Her hair is a wild mess, she has dried blood coating her skin from the top of her nose all the way down to her chest, and her wedding dress is a bloody nightmare. She looks like a bride from a Stephen King novel.

But even still, I wouldn't want anyone else.

She's *mine*.

That word reverberates through my body as I stare at her. She's my mate. The one I've been waiting for. The one I've been dying to touch and hold and kiss.

And she's finally here.

"I need to get you warm," I tell her, trying to keep my voice calm and soothing. She doesn't fight me or say a word as I take the wedding dress off her, stripping her to her lacy white bra and underwear.

The sexy sight makes my chest tight, but I force myself to look away. To ignore it. To focus on her needs, and not my own.

I pick her up again and slide under the blankets with her. She's ice cold.

We cling to each other for several long minutes as the heat from my body engulfs her, slowly thawing her out.

"You're going to be okay," I whisper, willing her body to warm up. "You're safe now."

I'm trying really hard to focus on the warming her up part and not on the incredible way her body feels pressed so closely to mine. Her soft breasts are pushing against my chest and it's taking every ounce of self-control I have to hold back a hungry groan.

There will be time for that later, I tell myself. *Be what she needs right now.*

After a while, her body doesn't feel so frigid anymore. It relaxes. It thaws.

I hear the water trickling onto the floor of the bathroom and I force myself to let her go.

"I'll be right back," I say before hurrying to the bathroom. I turn off the tap, empty some of the hot bath, and clean up the spilled water before I go and get her.

I'm shocked to see her sitting up in the bed. She has the blankets pulled up to her chest as she looks at me with some life in her eyes.

I nearly cry, I'm so relieved.

"Are you okay?" I ask as I rush over and drop to my knees in front of her.

She's looking at me like she's not sure if I'm real or a figment of her imagination.

"What happened?"

"How about you take a nice warm bath and then I'll explain everything?"

She just stares at me. "Okay."

She lets me carry her to the bathroom and then I put her feet on the ground. My traitorous eyes can't help but roam down her curves, taking in every tempting inch. She's so fucking sexy. I *need* her. My cock jolts and then starts to get hard, slowly rising as it points to the ceiling.

She spots it and then continues staring at it with enormous eyes. I snatch a towel off the hook and quickly wrap it around my waist.

"Why are you naked exactly?" she asks as she quickly looks away from the tent I'm pitching with the towel.

"Umm, I'll explain after the bath."

She looks at the bubbly water, noticing it for the first time. "Okay."

"Do you need help getting in?"

She swallows hard as she turns and looks at my chest. "I'll be alright," she whispers, her teeth no longer chattering.

"Okay," I say, "but I have to clean that wound on your nose. Slip into the bath and then I'll come in and clean it."

She doesn't say a word as I gently close the door and give her a minute. I can hear her taking her bra and panties off, which makes my hard cock rage even more.

I force myself to leave and I head into my room to grab some clothes. I get dressed in something nice—navy blue pants, a white t-shirt, and a thick gray woollen cardigan.

My rock hard dick is still very much noticeable in these pants, but there's not much I can do about that. I'm not going to lose this stubborn erection until I'm able to sink it into that girl's soft supple body. I'll just have to try and hide it the best I can.

I hurry back to the bathroom and listen at the door. The sound of water swishing tells me she's in the tub.

"I'm coming in," I say in a soft voice as I knock on the door.

She's lying in the tub with the bubbles up to her neck, watching me with an expression I can't quite read. I can't wait to know everything about her. I'm excited for the day that I know her so well that I can tell her mood by the way she walks into the room.

"I have to fix your nose," I whisper, not wanting to scare her. "I don't want it to get infected."

I don't have a first aid kit, since I heal so fast, but I do have some bandaids and disinfectant that my cousin left behind when she came to visit with her kid this summer. I grab it and bring it over to her.

"Does it hurt?" I ask as I grab a face cloth. I bunch it up and put my hand under the soapy water to wet it.

She sucks in a breath—I do too—when my hand is sharing the same water as her naked body.

"The cold froze it," she says as she looks at me wearily, "so it wasn't too bad. It's starting to hurt more now, though."

I dab it gently, wiping away some of the dried blood around it.

"It looks worse than it is," I tell her. I clean it up with the disinfectant and then put a bandaid over the worst part. It should take a few days, but it will heal. Her beautiful face will be back to flawless in no time.

"Thank you," she whispers when I'm all done.

I get up to leave, to give her some privacy, but she grabs my wrist and holds me there. "Can you stay with me?"

I sit back down on the tiles and nod. "As long as you need. I'm yours."

"What's your name?"

"Leo," I say.

"Like Leonardo the Ninja Turtle?"

I chuckle. "I prefer Leonardo Da Vinci the inventor."

"Oh, right." She shakes her head, embarrassed. I smile. "I'm Tara."

Tara.

I say the name over and over in my head, each time sounding more beautiful.

"What a way to end your wedding," I say, fishing for details. "Did you really get married today?"

My eyes dart to her ring finger, which is bare. Hopefully, that's a good sign.

"It didn't work out as planned," she whispers.

I'm waiting for her to go on, but she doesn't.

"So, what happened back there?" she finally asks. "Where did you come from?"

I tap her hand and then stand up. "Like I said, I'll explain *after* the bath. I'll leave you to it and go make you something warm to eat. I'm sure you need it."

I smile at her before heading to the door.

"Leo?" she says, that angelic voice stopping me in my tracks.

"Yeah?"

"Why are you being so nice to me?"

I take a deep breath as I gaze into her stunning eyes. How can I explain to her how I'm feeling? How happy and relieved I am that she's here? How obsessed I am with her even though I just learned her name? How can I tell her she means the world to me and one day soon, I'll mean the world to her?

How can I explain to her that everything will be different from now on?

That her world has just been split in two—the time before we met and the time after?

"I'll go make you something to eat," I say with a warm smile.

I exit the bathroom and leave her to finish up.

There is no explaining it. There are no words to describe the intensity of a mate's bond. They don't exist.

There's only showing. Only feeling.

And tonight, she'll see...

Tonight, she'll experience what it means to be mated to a grizzly shifter.

All. Night. Long.

Chapter Five

Tara

I step out of the draining bath and wrap a towel around me, feeling much much better. The blood is circulating through my body again. I can feel my toes.

I wiggle them on the wet mat, so thankful that I didn't lose any to frostbite. I love wearing flip-flops in the summer and some mangled missing toes would have seriously messed up my flip-flop game.

A warm shiver ripples through me when I remember how it felt to have Leo's big strong hand wrapped around them.

To be lying in his bed... My body flattened against his hard muscular frame... The sound of his heart beating to the same rhythm as mine... The feel of his warm breath on my neck... The kind words whispered into my ear, telling me that everything was going to be okay...

That man saved me.

I have no doubt about it.

I keep thinking about what happened and trying to put the pieces together. I've come up with a theory, but I'm nervous to ask him about it.

He left me a pile of clothes by the sink and I dry off and put them on. My bra and underwear need a good wash, so I leave those in the shower stall with my ruined bloody dress.

His pajama pants are way too big for me, so I tie the waist as tight as it will go and then roll them up my legs until I can finally see my feet. The t-shirt is huge as well, but it's Leo's so I'm already kind of in love with it. I'm already plotting how I can steal it.

It's a band I've never heard of—Stone Temple Pilots—and I can tell it's well-loved by the faded image. I sigh contently as I feel the soft material on my skin. The neck hole is so big that it falls over my shoulder, but it's kind of sexy at the same time, so I leave it.

I fix up my wet hair as best I can and then brush my teeth with a brand-new toothbrush he left me on the counter.

I would like to be wearing some makeup when he sees me for the first time not dressed as an axe-murdering bride, but I don't have any on me and his products are all for males.

Oh well, hopefully he has a thing for runaway brides or for really irresponsible drivers.

I take a deep breath and head out.

The warm inviting scent of hot soup wafts down the hallway and makes me moan.

I walk slowly down the hall, my bare feet silent on the hardwood floors, and smile when I arrive in the large open space that has Leo's adorable kitchen, his warm cozy living room with a roaring fire, and the dining area where I can picture us sitting over a hot meal and talking for hours.

Soft music is playing on the speakers—I recognize it as *Holocene* by Bon Iver—and Leo has his back turned to me, mixing something in the large pot.

He turns and looks at me with a warm beautiful smile as I walk in. It hits me right in the core and for some reason I want to start crying.

Not sad tears, the happy kind. An hour ago, I was alone in the snowstorm, I was trapped in a trunk, I was certain I was going to die, although I didn't know which traumatic way would get me.

And now I'm here. Safe and warm with this gorgeous man smiling at me, a crackling fire in the stunning stone fireplace, tender music, a hearty meal waiting for me, and all while the storm rages outside. The frigid wind is howling. The snow is accumulating on the windows. I'm so happy to be here with him, all snug and comfy in the safe shelter of his cabin. The only place I've ever felt this content and secure was at home as a kid.

It's a log cabin with giant logs towering up to the high A-framed ceiling and running horizontally along the walls. The lighting is soft and cozy with candles lit on every wooden shelf and on every piece of antique furniture. The large couches with folded flannel throw blankets draped over the backs of them are inviting me to sink into them and enjoy the warm fire.

Everything about this place is charming and delightful. It's so welcoming, especially when in stark contrast to the violent storm outside.

"Feel better?" he asks. He's so cute with his gray apron on, I can't even.

"*Much* better," I say, smiling back at him. "Thank you so much, Leo. I don't even know what to say."

"Then don't say anything," he says as he reaches into the cupboard and pulls out a bottle of wine. "Eat and drink instead."

I can't help but smile as I walk over and take a seat at the island while he opens the bottle. I could really use a drink. My eyes roam all over his hands and arms, free to take in the stunning view while he's distracted with the wine opener.

I want to run my hands up his thick woollen cardigan. I want to feel if the material is as soft as it looks. I want to feel if his biceps are as hard as they look.

He pulls the cork out with a pop and then pours each of us a glass of red wine.

I can't help but moan when I taste it. It's the best thing I've ever had.

"So," I say when we're looking at each other between sips. "I think I've put it together."

His eyebrow raises. "Oh yeah?"

He brings the wine glass to his lips and my breath catches when I see how big his arm is. He's so freaking hot. Like one-look-will-turn-you-into-a-psycho-stalker hot.

I push all that away and point at him. "*You* were the bear."

He takes a sip as he looks at me over the glass.

"You're one of those bear shifters," I say, pushing on before I lose the nerve. "Aren't you?"

"Bear shifters?"

"Yeah. I read an article about them."

"What did it say?"

"It talked about men who can turn into bears at will," I say, hoping I'm not sounding ridiculous right now. If the bear was just a coincidence, he's going to think I'm a total nut for bringing this up. "They're very strong and they heal fast. They're also very protective and loyal to their mates."

"Mates?"

"Yeah, they're monogamous their whole lives, saving themselves for their one true mate," I say, feeling my voice racing with excitement. "The bond of a shifter to his mate is unlike any other bond in nature. It's so intense that it only takes one sight or smell of the shifter's mate for him to know she's the one."

"Sounds pretty cool," he says all nonchalantly. Meanwhile, my heart is racing at the thought of it. When I read the article, I remember thinking it was the most beautiful thing I'd ever heard. I spent weeks dreaming of having a big burly bear shifter of my own.

"I thought so," I say, looking at my wine glass and feeling a little silly. "So, are you one?"

He takes a deep breath as he looks at me. That massive chest gets even bigger.

"I am."

"Really?" I say, staring at him in awe. "So, that grizzly bear that was trying to eat me? That was you?!"

He chuckles. "He wasn't trying to eat you. He was trying to save you."

I stare at his wide chest, wondering if his bear is looking at me now. Is he really in there?

"Have you... found your mate?"

"Yes."

My stomach sinks. I suddenly want to drink that entire wine bottle and crawl into bed.

"Oh," I say, my eyes dropping to the floor. "Cool. I'm happy for you."

This night just got a lot more disappointing. I glance at

the door expecting a stunning woman to walk in at any moment.

"What's her name?" I ask, not really wanting to know.

He smiles as he looks at me. "Tara."

This lucky bitch has the same name as me too? What the hell?

I'm *not* talking about this anymore. I might cry.

"That soup smells so good," I say, desperately trying to change the subject. "Did you make it?"

"I did," he says as he opens the cupboard. "Let me pour you a bowl."

I admire his big hulking back and nice round ass as he turns to the stove to fill it up. I know he's taken, but I still can't help crushing on him. The man saved me after all. That allows me to have a tiny little crush on him, doesn't it?

He pours two bowls and then carries them to the table, just gripping them with his bare hands even though they're probably scorching hot. I grab his wine glass and walk over to join him, sitting at the table across from him.

As I sit down, the violent wind increases and a tree rattles outside. I'm just so happy that I'm safe in here that I can't help but smile, even if this man and his stupid mate Tara just dumped a bucket of cold water on my sizzling desire.

We eat the soup in comfortable silence as the music plays and the fire crackles and pops.

I'm already feeling more comfortable with Leo than I ever did with my ex-fiancé. I'm glad I'm not with David right now. I'd probably be making excuses on why I couldn't consummate our wedding vows. 'I think the shrimp was bad. I'm going to be on the toilet *all* night. Rain-check?'

Instead, I'm with Leo, and there's no place on the planet I'd rather be.

"Why were you wearing a wedding dress?" he suddenly asks, his intense blue eyes locked on me.

Geez, is this guy a mind reader or something?

"I... a... I was... supposed to get... married."

He swallows hard as he watches me. His body is all tight and he's sitting up abnormally straight. "But you didn't, right?"

"No, I couldn't go through with it."

He lets out the breath he's holding and his body loosens. He whispers something under his breath that I can't quite catch, but I can sense the relief in his tone.

I don't know why he looks so relieved. He was probably worried that he'd have to deal with a jealous husband. No need to worry about that. David is probably just as relieved as I am that I skipped out on the nuptials.

"Who was the guy?" he asks with a bit of a sharp edge to his voice. "A boyfriend?"

"Not even," I say, shaking my head as I stir my soup. "My parents set me up with him. It was doomed from the start."

I go into the details of it, telling him all about David and how my mom wore me down into agreeing to marry him. About what a mistake it all was.

"I couldn't do it," I say, feeling awful about what I put everyone through. "My mom is going to be so mad that I ruined everything."

"You ruined one day of theirs," he says, his tone softer now. "Better that than ruining your whole life. I think that's a fair trade."

I tilt my head as his words bounce around inside my head. "I never thought of it like that."

He smiles. "That's what I'm here for."

We eat in silence for a little longer, and I'm shocked at

how comfortable it all is. My mind starts replaying the events of the night and I start to get a bad feeling in my stomach.

This man has a mate and we had many intimate moments. Too intimate for someone who's taken.

"How is your mate going to feel about... tonight?" I ask, feeling awful that I put both of them in this uncomfortable situation.

He smiles at me like he's in on a joke that I'm not. "What do you mean?"

"Well... We're here alone. Eating by candlelight. The music... The bath... And I saw your..."

His eyebrow raises.

"Little grizzly..." I say as I point to his crotch over the table.

"Little?" he says with a grin.

My cheeks burn so hot, I might burn this whole cabin down if I'm not careful.

"Sorry, it wasn't little," I blurt out, not quite knowing what I'm saying until it's too late. "It was quite... never mind. What did you put in this soup? Is that celery I taste?"

I'm staring at the bowl with wide eyes, cursing myself for being so damn embarrassing.

What was that?! *Get it together, girl!*

After a long, soul-crushing moment, I force my eyes up and look at him. He doesn't look mad or embarrassed. He looks amused, like he can't wait to hear what moronic thing I'll say next.

"So, is she going to be mad?"

"My mate?"

"Yeah."

"You tell me."

I sigh. She's going to be *pissed*. I know I would be if

some dumb broad got herself into trouble and then ended up seeing my man's naked cock, curled up with him in my bed to warm up, took a bath in front of him, and then spent the night alone with him by candlelight. I would be apocalyptic.

She's probably going to give me two black eyes to go along with my bloody nose.

And I'll deserve it.

"I think—"

The power goes out and I forget all about Leo's mate wanting to kill me. The lights turn off in the kitchen, the music stops, and the hum of the fridge dies down as we stare at each other in shock.

Only the gentle swaying light from the candles and the warm glow of the fire are lighting up the room.

And my host looks more gorgeous than ever.

Chapter Six

Leo

The sight of this girl at my kitchen table bathed in candlelight is filling me with a majestic awe. It's hard to take my eyes off her. I don't want to look away.

I can't believe I told my brothers that I didn't need her. That I would be fine without my mate. That I would be okay without this mesmerizing girl in my life.

One look at her smiling shyly while eating her soup is enough to know that I was a complete and utter fool.

I need her. I need her more than I need to eat. More than I need to breathe.

I need her like I haven't needed anything before.

My heart beats for her. Our souls are connected.

My mate is in my life now and there's no going back.

"How long do you think we'll lose power for?" she asks as she looks around the dark room.

"It won't come back until the storm is over at least," I say, only looking at her. Those green eyes are entrancing. "It might even be a few days."

"Is your mate okay?" she asks as she pulls my t-shirt up a little higher on her chest.

I fight back a growl when I see her round breasts jiggling with the movement. She's not wearing a bra and it's driving me crazy.

"Is she traveling in the storm? Is she coming back tonight?"

This poor girl. I know she must feel the draw to me, just as I'm feeling it for her. It must be torture for her to think her mate is taken. To think that there's someone else. I know because I felt those same torturous thoughts when I saw her in a wedding dress.

"Tara," I say in a soft voice.

Her back straightens as she looks at me. "Yeah?"

"I thought it was strange that my grizzly bear wanted to wander around in the middle of the worst blizzard in the past decade," I say, keeping my eyes on hers. "But then I realized, it was fate guiding us along. Pushing us into the storm."

"Totally," she says, nodding as she stares back at me with focused green eyes. "Wait, what?"

"My mate was out there, in danger, and I had to save her."

"Your mate was in the storm?" she says, darting to her feet. "Is she still there? Should we go look for her? Oh shit, I'm sorry that I distracted you from finding her! What should we do?"

I can't help but smile as I look at her starting to panic. She's fucking adorable.

"Tara," I say softly as I tilt my head forward and raise my eyebrows.

"What? Oh..."

It sinks in.

"Oh!"

She slides back into the chair, but her body is all tense as she stares at me.

"*I'm* your Tara?"

I nod. "You're my Tara. You're my mate."

"*Oh...*"

She stares at me for a long while as a million thoughts race through her mind.

Her eyes suddenly narrow on me skeptically. "How can you be so sure?"

"I've never been more sure of anything in my life."

She nibbles her bottom lip as she considers it and the sexy sight makes me groan involuntarily.

"Well, I'm not sold on the matter," she finally says. "You're going to have to prove it."

"Alright."

I take a deep breath as I stand up. Her alert green eyes follow me as I move around the table and walk right up to her.

I gently take her jaw in my big hand, slowly lean down, and I kiss her.

She moans as her lips part for me. The tip of her tongue teases mine.

God, her mouth is so soft. I could do this all night.

I slide my tongue against hers, tasting her sweetness, and sinking into this beautiful moment that I know I'll cherish forever.

Her hand slides up my arm as she opens her lips wider. I kiss her deeper.

If this doesn't prove it to her, then I don't know what will.

Only mates can kiss like this.

When I finally pull away, her eyes are closed, her chin is tilted up, and her lips are pursed like she wasn't ready for me to stop.

Those eyelids slowly open as I stand back up. Glossy green eyes look up at me like her whole world has just shifted and she's suddenly realizing her life will never be the same.

"Okay," she says in a breathless tone. "That proves it."

I smile as I pull out the chair beside her and sit down.

She turns to face me. I take her hand, swallowing it in my own as we gaze into each other's eyes.

"So, there's no one else?" she asks in a whisper. "It's only me?"

I nod.

"And you've never...?"

I shake my head.

"*Ever?*"

"No, Tara," I say as my grip on her hand tightens. "I've been waiting for you all my life. You're the only one I want."

"I haven't either," she says, and the bit of tight dread that's been lingering in my chest since I saw her in her wedding dress disappears. "I'm a virgin too. I didn't realize it, but I guess I was waiting for you as well."

I want her more than ever.

She moans as I lean in and kiss her again, harder this time, letting her know how much I appreciate her saving that sweet little cherry for me. I'll never forget it.

We stay like this for a long time, kissing slowly and tenderly like we have all night. We do have all night. We have a lifetime together.

I wonder if she realizes that she's never leaving. That our lives are interconnected in the most intimate way now. That there's no going back.

"Come," I say as I take her hand and pull her to the fireplace where we can be more comfortable.

She sits cross-legged on the rug, watching me with excited eyes as I take a blanket and drape it over her shoulders.

"Thank you," she whispers as she wraps herself up in it.

The orange flickering light from the fire is reflecting in her eyes and I'm suddenly wishing it never stops snowing. That we get snowed in here forever.

"I love your place," she says as I sit down. "It's so cute."

"It's going to feel like home soon," I say, wondering if I'm moving too fast. "Where do you live?"

"I live in Pocatello with my parents. It's in Idaho. They want me to move out so they can move to Argentina. That's why they were trying to marry me off, so I'd leave."

"You're welcome to live here," I say, hoping I don't sound too desperate. "I'd love to see you every day."

She doesn't answer, but she does get a big wide smile on her face.

"What's life like here?" she asks. "What do you do?"

I tell her all about my brothers and how we grew up here on the mountain. I have her laughing at all of the crazy stories and the sound just makes me so damn happy. I'm still in shock that she's actually here in front of me.

"Michael was the adrenaline junkie," I tell her as she laughs. "He was wild back then. Oliver and I could get him to do *anything* on a dare. Once, I dared him to walk his grizzly bear through the grocery store and he did it! People ran out of there screaming their heads off. There was fruit *everywhere*. The manager ran to his truck to get his shotgun, and me and Oliver had to wrestle it out of his hands. Michael is still banned from the place. He has to get his groceries in the next closest town, about an hour away."

"I can't wait to meet them," she says as she takes another sip of her wine. I refill her glass and mine too.

"You'll meet them soon enough," I promise her. "They're going to be shocked to see you."

She smiles as she looks at her glass. "What do you do for work?"

I shrug. "The three of us work construction in the summer. We have our own business, designing and building houses and commercial buildings around town. Did you happen to see the post office on your way in?"

"I saw snow, ice, and more snow," she says with a laugh.

"Right. Well, we built it."

"I'm sure it's beautiful."

"Not as beautiful as you."

Her cheeks turn a dark shade of pink as she smiles shyly at me. "I guess, if you're into big bandages in the middle of someone's face."

"I'm into you."

Our lips come together like we're already on the same page.

I kiss this perfect angel, wondering if I'll ever get tired of these lips, but knowing that I never will.

That would be impossible.

This mouth was made for me.

Chapter Seven

Tara

I don't know what time it is, but I'm not ready for bed.

Leo carries the large mattress into the living room and places it on the floor in front of the fireplace. I fix up the sheets, wondering who this bed is for. Me? Him? Me *and* him?

I'm not sure, but one of those options is awfully intriguing.

I feel silly for not making the connection before, especially since it was pretty obvious now that I'm looking back on it. What was I thinking? He told me his mate's name was Tara and I was like 'Duh, that's my name too!'

He must think I'm a total moron.

But come on. I had no idea that an amazing man like *this* could be into a girl like *me*. That doesn't happen very often, so I can't be too hard on myself for not even contemplating the fact that we could be made for one another.

I guess this proves that sometimes the universe will single you out, get your back, and move mountains for you. It will give you something so good that you wouldn't have even dared to dream it up in the first place.

My neck begins tingling as I watch him fluff up the pillows and place them on the mattress. I brush my fingertips over the skin under my ear and the tingling gets stronger. The sensation is a demanding one. It's like an itch I can't scratch. Like the vibrating area is missing something.

"It's going to get cold tonight," Leo says as he tosses another log into the fire. I can't help but gawk at his broad shoulders. They're perfectly round. I'll never be stuck behind a tall guy at a concert again. I can just hop onto these babies and I'll have a front-row view no matter where we are. "But the fire should keep you warm."

"You mean it should keep *us* warm, right?"

He looks at me with a hungry look in his eyes.

"I mean..." I quickly say with my heart pounding. "I don't want you to have to sleep in a cold room all by yourself. That's not really fair. I wasn't implying that..."

The hunger in his eyes intensifies and it makes the words dry up in my throat. What was I implying? That we should sleep in the same bed?

My brain starts to do some mental gymnastics to justify why that's the only suitable option.

"Well, we are mates," I say with an innocent little shrug. "We can sleep in the same bed without doing anything, right?"

His lustful eyes roam up and down my body and I suddenly realize how stupid that suggestion is. The second we get into that bed, we're going to be all over each other.

The thought of that sends my tingling neck into a frenzy. *What the hell is that? Did I hurt it in the accident?*

"We'll sleep together," he says with a finality in his tone. "I want to make sure you're warm all night."

I swallow hard as I look at him and nod. "Sure, I mean, if that's what you think is best."

My fingertips brush over the tingling spot on my neck and he notices. He lets out a low possessive growl as he watches. It's almost as if he knows what's going on with my body and I don't.

I choke a little when I spot the long hard erection running along his muscular thigh. This man's cock is *huge*.

I saw it.

I still can't believe that thing was real. It was out in the cold *and* it was that massive? Was that *with* shrinkage?? How big is it going to look in a warm room?

It might not be long before I find out... That is both terrifying and exciting at the same time. Mostly exciting.

I'm busy thinking about his penis when I realize that he's waiting for me to answer a question.

"What?"

"I asked you what you're thinking about," he says with a gorgeous smile. "You keep nibbling on your bottom lip."

"Oh, um... birds."

"Birds?"

"Yeah, and a... migratory patterns."

He nods his head as he looks at me. I force out a smile, hoping I don't look deranged. "You know, because of the snow. I'm hoping the birds are all okay."

He smiles like I'm not a deranged lunatic and like that's a perfectly normal thing to be thinking about right now.

"What are you thinking about?" I ask him.

He drops his beautiful blue eyes onto his wine glass and my breath catches in my throat. He's so gorgeous. It's hard to think about anything else when he's sitting in front of me like this. I wonder if he's this stunning to everyone or if it's just me since we're mates.

No. It can't be just me. With that big muscular body and that beautiful face, he's a ten on ten no matter who is looking at him.

He looks at me with those deep thoughtful eyes and I shiver.

"I was just thinking..." he says, unsure of how to say it. "Of how I can express my gratitude. To you."

"To me?" I say, nearly choking. "Um, you're the one who saved me about ten times in one night! You're the one letting me crash your party. You're the one who bathed me, fed me, and is letting me sleep in your place. I should be the one thanking you!"

He smiles.

"Thank you," I say shyly. "By the way."

"That's nothing," he says with a dismissive shrug. "Thank you, Tara, for not getting married. Thank you for running out on that wedding. I can't imagine how hard that must have been to do."

"Oh," I say, feeling my cheeks heating up. "It was hard. But there was no way I could have married him. I don't know, I just felt..."

"Something stronger calling to you?"

I nod as I gaze into his warm eyes. "Yeah."

"That was our bond. It will only get stronger over time."

"Really?" I say with a chuckle. "Because it's already pretty strong."

He moves in with those sexy lips and my whole body starts tingling. His hand cups the side of my face and he pulls me to his mouth. I moan when his soft warm mouth touches mine.

He's a wonderful kisser. You'd think someone as big and

strong as Leo would be firm and rough, but he's tender and gentle, handling me like I'm the most precious, delicate thing alive.

My head is spinning when he pulls away and gazes into my eyes.

"It's time for bed," he whispers as he starts kissing my neck. The demanding spot under my ear is tingling like crazy with his lips so close.

"You'll stay with me?" I ask in a breathless tone as those magical lips kiss along my bare shoulder. "I don't want to sleep alone."

"You'll never sleep alone again," he promises.

A weight feels like it's lifted off my chest. I just want this man with me, forever.

I grab onto his arms and pull him on top of me as I lay down on the mattress. He keeps most of his weight off me, but leaves just enough to turn me on even more.

I'm not wearing any underwear under the clothes he leant me and my body is acutely aware of that fact. My nipples are rock hard as they rub on the inside of his old t-shirt, and my pussy is *aching* with need under his pajama pants.

I need him so badly. I want him *in* me... I want him to *own* me...

I'm holding the back of his neck as he kisses me in front of the crackling fire. It's so warm in here. So sexy. The air is filled with heat and I feel like my body might implode it's burning so hot.

My desperate hands claw at his shirt, trying to pull it off.

He suddenly takes his mouth away from mine, sits up, and grins at me as he pulls his shirt off in one smooth motion.

"*Holy...*" I whisper as I stare at his naked torso in awe. It's a mosaic of muscles. A vast massive chest with a perfectly defined six-pack underneath. His shoulders are even sexier without a t-shirt covering them, and his arms... My god, his arms... I want to start a fan club for them. I'll write them fan mail every day.

Dear arms,
I can stare at you for hours.
Your greatest fan,
Tara.

He tosses his shirt onto the couch and I let out a little moan when I see his hard gorgeous muscles clenching and tightening with every movement he makes. I'm hypnotized by him. He's unreal.

That sexy grin is back when he sees me shamelessly gawking at his body.

"It's all yours, baby," he says as he grabs my wrist and puts my trembling hand on his stomach. I hold my breath as I touch his flexed abs, marveling at how hard they are and how good they feel. My pussy is burning as I slide my hand up to his chest and explore every inch of it.

"You like that?" he growls.

I nod my head, unable to find any words to describe what I'm feeling.

"You can touch me," he says as he slides his hands under my t-shirt and up my sides, "*whenever* and *wherever* you want."

I drop my hands with a heavy moan as his palms slide up and he cups my bare breasts.

"*Oh,*" I moan as my eyes close and my back arches. It feels so good. How can it feel so damn good?

"*Yes,*" I gasp as he takes my shirt and pulls it up. I lift my shoulders to make it easier for him and my shirt slips off my head, never to be seen again. My breasts tumble free as I lay back down with my firm nipples tingling.

Now, it's his turn to gawk at me. He's staring at my chest with a possessive hunger in his eyes. I'm all his. I know it now.

It's the first time a man has seen me without a top on and I'm surprised at how much I like it. I want him to see me. I want him to see everything. I'm craving it badly.

"You are so fucking perfect," he growls before dropping down and dragging that hot tongue over my hard nipple. Those big warm hands cup my breasts and Leo is all over them, licking, sucking, and kissing every inch of my chest.

I slide my hands into his soft hair and moan as he moves from one breast to the other, making me breathless. It's like he knows just how to move his tongue to draw out the pleasure and make my body react.

My hips start rolling and I suddenly whimper when my leg touches his erection. It feels long, hard, and oh so tantalizingly *thick*.

He's sucking on my nipple and driving me wild as I reach down and touch it. He moans heavily as I slide my palm down his firm length. It feels even bigger in my hand. And I know it's going to feel even larger in my pussy. I have no idea how this monster is going to fit inside me at all.

But I keep rubbing it until he kisses down my bare stomach and I can no longer reach it.

"Don't worry," he growls as his fingers curl into the waistband of my pajama pants. "You'll be able to touch it all you want soon. But right now, I'm *dying* to put my mouth on you."

"*Oh god*," I whisper as the fire roars behind us. This is it. This is the moment when I get naked in front of a man for the first time.

Leo's hungry eyes are feasting on my body as he grips my pants and slowly pulls them down. He holds his breath as they slip over my thighs and my small tuft of pubic hair is revealed. I can tell his mouth is watering as he pulls my pants down my calves and off of my feet.

I want him to see it, I want to please him, but I'm still shy, so I keep my legs closed.

But Leo isn't having any of that.

With a demanding growl, he takes my knees in his big hands and pries my legs open. An excited thrill ripples through me when I see his eyes darken with lust. He's staring right at my naked pussy and I'm loving every second of it.

"*Fuck*," he whispers under his breath as he stares shamelessly at my virgin sex. "You are perfect. Pink, tight, and *perfect*."

He drops down and I dart up onto my elbows.

"What are you... *oh!*"

His hot tongue hits and all of my worries and self-conscious thoughts melt away. They're replaced with this indescribable feeling of pure unwavering bliss as his tongue moves over me.

I'm willingly spreading my legs now. I'm stretching them wide open, so consumed by lust as he tastes me that I'm no longer worried about this being my first time.

His lips and tongue are moving all over my sex, making me feel like I'm falling. I grab two fistfuls of the blankets and hold on for dear life.

"*Oh*," I whimper when I feel his hot tongue sliding into my wet entrance. He drags it up to my throbbing clit and my hips start rolling against him when he sucks on it.

My breath is coming out in short rapid gasps of air. My

back keeps arching. My blood is boiling with unquenchable lust and desire.

Those strong hands are gripping the inside of my thighs, holding my legs open as he devours my pussy. His fingertips hurt, but it's only amping up my arousal.

"*Yes!*" I cry out when I feel his finger penetrating me. "*Oh, Leo...*"

I force my eyes open and moan when I see the sexy sight of this gorgeous man between my legs. He's burying his face between my thighs, tongue moving up my wet folds before he wraps his lips around my clit and sucks hard.

He adds another thick finger inside me and slides them both in deep.

I cry out as my pussy clamps down on him, both of us probably wondering how his giant cock is going to fit in there if his two fingers feel this tight.

But it's not time to worry about that.

It's time to enjoy every incredible sensation this man is giving me. Every delicious stroke of his tongue, every intoxicating curl of his finger, and every hungry possessive groan, which tells me that this is only the beginning...

Chapter Eight

Leo

I'm in heaven as I glide my tongue up this girl's sweet, silky little slit. I slide my tongue between her pink folds and taste her honey with a hungry groan.

She's writhing on the mattress now, getting into it as she coats my mouth with her warm juices. Her pussy is dripping wet.

My cock is aching it's so hard, but I'm not ready to pull away just yet. I want her to cum on my mouth. I want to taste this sweet little cunt while it's cumming.

"*Oh, Leo,*" she moans in a desperate tone as I play with her hard little clit. "Oh, right there. Don't stop..."

I slide my hands onto her ass and pull her to my face, sucking on her clit until she's screaming.

My cock is *throbbing* with the sexy sounds she's making. I've never been this turned on.

I force my eyes open and look at the sexy view in front

of me. Tara's back is arched with her delicious little tits thrust into the air. Her beautiful face is twisted up in pleasure, her hands gripping the pillow beside her head.

I'm in love with her already. In love and utterly obsessed.

There's nothing I wouldn't do to protect her. Nothing I wouldn't do to make her mine.

My mate is finally here and she's not going anywhere.

Two of my fingers are lodged inside her and I'm curling them to hit her G spot.

"*Oh shit*," she cries out when I find it. She grinds her cunt on my lips, rubbing her clit against my mouth as I stroke her from the inside.

"I'm going to cum," she cries out with a sudden urgency. "I'm going to cum!"

I pull my fingers out, bury my tongue in her tight little virgin hole, and moan as her whole body shakes. She screams out my name as her pussy cums all over my mouth.

Fucking hell... This girl... She's so goddamn fucking perfect.

I let out a possessive growl as I lick her through it, tasting her sweetness as her body explodes into trembles. Her legs shake on the sides of my head as she whimpers and moans.

Mark her.

It's my bear. I've been ignoring him until now, but he's becoming louder and more demanding.

Claim her. Mark her.

There are no words in my head, but his intentions are *very* clear. He wants this girl claimed, bred, and marked. And he wants it *now*.

Leave me alone, I warn him.

He growls back at me.

Tara is still moaning on the bed as I sit up and wipe my mouth. She's grabbing her tits and writhing as the last of the orgasm works its way through her veins.

I drag my eyes up her naked body until it's on the spot destined for my mark.

Below her ear. On her neck. My bear lets out a possessive growl as I look at it.

Every bear shifter marks their mate. It lets every man on the planet know that this girl is off-limits. Other bear shifters can see it and they'll stay away.

But it works on human men too. They might not be able to see it with their inferior eyes, but they'll be able to sense that this woman is claimed and spoken for. They'll leave her alone if they know what's good for them.

My mouth waters as my eyes linger on the spot.

There's nothing I want more than to mark this beauty, but I can't do it right now. I'll scare the poor girl away if I chomp down on her neck. I'm worried she'll run and skip out on me the same way she skipped out on that poor schmuck she left standing at the altar.

My grizzly bear doesn't like where my mind is. He wants her marked and he doesn't care what happens after.

He growls as he tries to claw his way out. I flex my body, squeeze my eyes shut, and push him back down.

Fuck off. Not happening.

He snarls at me.

I said, fuck off.

He grumbles and starts pacing around angrily.

"What is it?" Tara asks in a whisper. "What's wrong?"

I force my eyes open to find her kneeling in front of me, her worried face in front of mine.

I'm about to make up a lie, but then I remember I'm

talking to my mate and we don't have to keep anything between us.

"My bear," I say with a hoarseness in my voice. "He's starting to act up."

"Oh," she says as she drops her eyes to my chest. "Is there anything I can do?"

I shake my head as I gaze at her with a loving look. "I just need to settle him down."

She slides her hand down my arm and then drags her palm along my muscular thigh. My cock jolts at having her hand so close to it.

"Maybe I can help you... settle down," she says as she licks her lips and lowers her body.

Before I can say anything, she's reaching into my pants and wrapping her warm hand around my rock hard cock.

My head drops back and I let out a deep moan as she gives it a squeeze.

"You're..." I moan. "You're..."

She pulls my cock out, opens her mouth, and slides it inside.

"You're... fucking amazing."

My whole body melts as she runs her silky little tongue up my hard shaft.

It silences my grizzly bear. I feel him settling down with a frustrated grumble.

With him out of the way, I can fully focus on the incredible sensation of my mate's mouth on my cock. She squeezes her lips around me and moves her head up and down, coating my erection with her soft tongue.

She cups my balls with her free hand as she sucks me off. They must be so heavy. They've been filling up since I first laid eyes on her, getting ready for the moment when I slide my cock into her cunt and breed her sexy little body.

Every drop of seed waiting in there is destined for her womb. I want to cum in her mouth, but that's going to have to wait for another time. This load is here to breed my mate.

Tara keeps making these sexy moans as she slides up and down my dick. I sink my hands into her auburn hair and grab a fistful of it.

"You like sucking on your mate's big cock?" I growl as I guide her head up and down.

She pulls me out of her mouth and looks up at me with lustful green eyes. "*Yes*," she moans. "I love it so much."

I'm feasting my eyes on her naked body as she takes me back into her mouth. The curve of her spine leads to her beautiful round ass. I wish I could see beyond that. I want to see what her pussy looks like when she's bent over like this.

I make a mental note to buy lots of mirrors. I need mirrors all over this bedroom so I can see my sexy girl from every single angle.

She starts jerking me off while sucking on my head and the feeling is so good that I know I have to stop her. I want to stop her. I try to stop her.

But, I can't.

It feels too good. I drown in the moment and before I know it, an orgasm is rushing forward.

"Open your mouth," I growl as I grab my cock.

She quickly sits on her heels, puts her hands on my thighs, opens her mouth, and looks up at me with the sexiest look imaginable.

"That's it," I growl as I stroke myself a couple of times. "Just like that."

I point the head of my cock into her mouth and unleash a thundering orgasm that has my body shaking.

She moans with pleasure as stream after stream of hot

cum leaves my cock and lands on her tongue. Those sexy green eyes never leave mine as she swallows most of me down. The rest spills out onto her lips and chin.

"*Mmmmm,*" she moans once the surging stops. She licks her lips and takes my cock back, stroking and sucking it as I try to snap myself back into reality.

"That's my girl," I growl as I cup the back of her head. "You know just how to please me, baby girl."

My cock is still as hard as steel. Her mouth feels divine, but I'm ready to move on and test her little pussy out.

"On your back," I command.

She slides my dick out of her mouth and watches me with those glossy green eyes as she lies down in front of me.

I grip my cock and lean over her, pressing my thick head to her tight virgin entrance.

"You ready for it?" I ask in a hoarse tone. I can't believe this moment is finally here. I'm about to claim my mate for good. This morning, I wasn't sure if it would ever happen and now, here I am, on the cusp of sliding into my mate's beautiful soaking-wet pussy.

"I'm ready for you, Leo," she says with a moan. "I want it so bad."

I kiss her soft lips and thrust in with one firm drive of my hips. She cries into my mouth as I penetrate her deeply, taking her cherry and claiming her warm juicy cunt.

"Oh god," she cries out in short gasps. "*Oh god.*"

I want to comfort her with tender words and soft kisses, but I'm gritting my teeth as her pussy clamps down on my cock so tightly I can't think straight.

It's all I can focus on. She's so unbelievably *tight*.

I wrap my arms around her and start rocking my hips, easing in and out of her an inch at a time.

"It's so *deep*," she moans as she moves her head to the side, exposing her neck.

My inner grizzly growls when I gaze down at the spot under her ear.

Stop, I warn him. I look away, not wanting to get him started, and stare at her swaying tits instead. They're bouncing around with every thrust I give her.

Her pussy is taking me in easier now and I pick up the pace, fucking her with longer harder strokes.

"You feel so good," I moan as her hot little pussy pulses and milks my shaft.

I look down and curse under my breath when I see the beautiful sight of her pink virgin cream coating my shaft.

I'm not wearing a condom. We have nothing stopping us from uniting in the best possible way. One load from me and this beauty will be pregnant. She'll have my seed growing in her womb for the next nine months.

That's what I want more than anything. I want her bred with my cubs. I want to fuck a baby into her.

"Come here," I say as I grab her hips and pick her up. I lay down on the mattress and place her straddling me with my hard dick still lodged deep inside her cunt.

"Ride me," I growl. "Show me how much you love my cock."

She plants her knees on the mattress and starts moving her soft pussy up and down my length. Her tits are hanging over my face, sending a wave of possessiveness surging through my body. These beautiful tits are mine. This girl is *mine*.

"That's my sexy girl," I say as I watch her taking every inch. "Just like that, baby girl. Up and down on my big cock. Your pussy feels incredible."

She starts making these sexy little moans and whimpers

69

as she rides me higher and faster. I grab her hips and start thrusting up every time she comes down.

"*Oh,*" she whimpers as I push in *deep.*

"That's it," I growl. "This cock was made for you, sexy girl. It was made for your tight little pussy. Yours only. It will only ever be inside of you, I promise."

She lunges down and kisses me hard, shoving her tongue down my throat as she fucks my cock. I'm so in love. I can't get enough of my mate.

Her quick whimpers turn into deep moans and I can tell she's close to cumming.

Knowing she's about to erupt, makes me ready too. I won't be able to hold back when her virgin cunt is cumming on my dick. Is there ever going to be a better feeling than that?

Breed her.

It's my bear with another one of his selfish demands. Only this time, we're on the same page.

I will, I growl back to him.

"You're going to cum when I tell you to," I say in a deep commanding voice. "Understand?"

"*Yes,*" she moans as she bounces up and down on my cock. "It's coming..."

"Not until I give the word," I growl as I grip her ass cheeks and spread them apart.

Her eyes are squeezed closed and her mouth is open as she rides me. Silky locks of auburn hair bounce on her shoulders. She's so fucking gorgeous.

"When I count down from three," I say as I sit up. "I want you to sink down on my cock, rub your clit on me, and cum *hard.*"

"*Oh, Leo...*"

"Three."

She digs her nails into my shoulders and fucks me faster.

"Two."

Her hard nipples are grazing my face as she bounces on my dick. We're so close... I'm seconds from filling her womb with my seed... Moments from breeding her...

"One."

She sinks down on me, throws her head back while rubbing her clit on my pelvis, and screams as she cums *hard*.

I thrust my hips up, getting my cock as close to her womb as I can, and release with a carnal roar. Her tight virgin pussy squeezes and pulses around my shaft as I unload my seed deep into her with surge after surge of hot cum.

When the screaming stops, she whimpers and trembles against my chest. I wrap my arms around her and hold her tightly while her womb takes every drop.

"You're mine now," I whisper as I breathe in her delicious scent. "Now and forever."

"What took so long?" she whispers back.

I grin as I rest my forehead on her shoulder and focus on the amazing moment. The feeling of being connected, of knowing she's mine, of being inside her where I belong. It's the best night of my life. There isn't even a close second.

The only thing trying to ruin it is my bear, but I won't let him. He grumbles in annoyance as he finally settles down, knowing I'm not going to mark her neck right now.

He's just going to have to be patient.

We waited this long for her to arrive, we can wait a little longer to put our mark on her.

Although, I hope I don't have to wait too long.

I want it too.

Desperately.

Chapter Nine

Tara

I wake up to a loud vicious growl.

"What was that?" I gasp as I dart up, instantly awake. I hold the blankets over my bare chest as I look around in a panic.

It sounded like there's a monster in the room.

Leo is sitting on the side of the mattress with his naked back to me. He's slumped over with his head in his hands. Every muscle in his large back is stretched tight. He looks larger than before. Like he's swelled up in size if that's possible.

"Leo?" I whisper as the flickering light from the fire causes shadows to dance on his skin. The wind is roaring outside. "Are you okay?"

"I..." he says in a growly monstrous tone. "*I*... I didn't want you to see me like this."

"Like what?" I ask, trying to keep the shakiness out of my voice. "Tell me what's happening."

I put my hand on his back and he flinches.

"It's okay," I whisper. "You can trust me. I'm your mate, remember?"

He's breathing heavily, those big shoulders and that flexed back moving up and down violently. The grunts and growls he's making are like nothing I've ever heard from him before. Something is wrong. I can tell.

"Please don't keep it from me," I whisper as I run my hand along his spine. "Please..."

He huffs out an aggressive breath and then slowly turns around.

"*Oh,*" I gasp when I see his face. It's not the same face I fell in love with this evening. His forehead is unnaturally large, his jaw longer and distorted. His front canines look monstrous with the way they're pressing out against his upper lip. I can see the tips of sharp fangs sticking out.

He looks like he's doubled in size and there are spots on his body that have brown hair sticking out. I don't remember him being so hairy before.

All of that is shocking, but it's his eyes that are the most eerie. They're shining a bright golden color as they pierce me with a possessive look.

It would be natural to be scared, to want to run away, but I don't. I feel more drawn to him than ever. My heart goes out to him. All I want is to end his pain.

Even looking like this, he's beautiful to me. He's gorgeous.

"What is it?" I whisper. "What can I do to help?"

Those golden eyes glance at the tingling spot on my neck. The sensation of being incomplete becomes urgent, demanding. I feel this intense craving to be marked ripping through my body. I... I... I don't know what's happening.

"Is it this?" I whisper as I touch the aching spot.

His lips pull back, revealing his fangs. He growls low as his eyes shine.

"Your lips go here," I say as it starts to click into place. "Don't they?"

"*Yes*," he says in a low inhuman growl.

Something from that shifter article I read years ago returns to my mind. The mark. Bear shifters mark their mates.

That's why my neck is tingling so much. That's why it feels like I'm incomplete.

"Mark me, Leo," I whisper as I let the blankets fall from my chest. "Mark your mate. I can handle it."

He lets out a low possessive grumble as he looks at my naked breasts.

I lay down on the mattress and spread my legs for him.

With a low snarl, he climbs on top of me.

"*Whoa*," I whisper when I see the size of his cock. His shoulders and chest aren't the only parts of him that are bigger.

The mattress dips under his weight. His enormous body stretches my legs open until it hurts.

"Mark me," I beg, urging him on. I'm doing this for him. For us. I want us to be one. "Do what you have to do."

I reach down and grab his firm cock as he eyes my neck with those golden eyes.

"*Oh*," I moan as I put him inside me. He pushes in until he's rooted firmly in my aching pussy. I feel so *full*. So complete.

He growls as he licks my neck. I turn my head to the side, giving him full access as he begins to thrust in and out, owning my pussy with his massive dick. I scream loudly with every hard punishing thrust. He's so *thick*. He's so big.

He's not taking it slow and gentle like before. The carnal part of him is in control now. The monster is running the show.

He grabs my hip and his sharp claws dig into my flesh without piercing it. I cry out as he pulls me closer, tilting my body to thrust in deeper.

"*Yes*," I moan when I feel his sharp fangs dragging along my neck. "Bite me. Mark me. I want to feel it."

He lunges forward with a snarl and sinks his teeth into the spot. I scream out as I feel his mark taking hold on me.

It sets me off. My pussy erupts around his thick thrusting cock. I cum so hard it stuns me. Tears flood my eyes as desperate cries rip out of my throat.

Leo removes his fangs and kisses the bloody spot.

My whole body is shaking violently as the fierce orgasm surges through my veins. I feel so close to him. I feel like I'm his.

He hits me with three hard thrusts and then roots himself in deep. I moan in ecstasy when I feel him cumming deep inside me. His body shudders in my arms. He groans in my ear.

We cling to each other for several long seconds until the intensity wains and we both start trembling.

His tight body goes slack. I feel more of his weight on me as he relaxes. I scratch his back, still not quite believing the difference the mark has made.

We're one now. We're truly one. It feels like my soul has been reunited with its other half. Like it didn't know it was incomplete until now.

I'm finally whole.

Leo's body begins to shrink back down to its normal

size. I groan as he pulls out of me and rolls off. He's breathing heavily as he stares at me in awe.

"Ow," I moan when I close my legs. I didn't realize how far apart they were stretched.

He's on me at once, stroking my hair and gazing at me with his worried blue eyes. "Are you okay, my love? Did I hurt you?"

I shake my head as I gaze up at him, feeling closer to him than I've ever felt to anyone. "No," I whisper. "You could never hurt me."

He kisses my lips. I close my eyes and focus on the beautiful feeling of being so connected.

Of being his.

I reach up and touch his mark. The spot is no longer tingling. It's no longer demanding.

It feels whole. Complete.

Just like us.

Chapter Ten

Tara

"Good morning," I whisper as I curl into Leo's big warm arms. He wraps them around me and holds me tight. This is by far the best way to wake up.

"Did you sleep well?" he asks in a deep groggy voice that's just so freaking adorable. His hair is all messy and his eyes are a little puffy. I just want to kiss him, but I don't because in the morning my mouth is a toxic waste dump before I brush my teeth.

"I did," I say as I rest my cheek on his big chest. I can hear his heart beating in a slow relaxed rhythm. It makes me want to stay in bed all day.

The mattress is so comfy and the sheets are so soft. We still don't have power and it's still snowing outside, but we have all we need here.

"How come the fire is still going?" I ask when I see it roaring. It should be nothing but ashes by now.

"I woke up every hour to throw in another log."

He just says it so casually. Like it's nothing.

"You did that... for me?"

I'm so touched I feel like I might cry.

"I didn't want you to get cold," he says with a shrug.

That's one of the nicest things anyone has ever done for me. I stare up at him in awe until he kisses my forehead.

"Thank you," I whisper with a smile as I lay back down on his chest. "Is there something I can do to repay you?"

"You don't have to repay me for taking care of you," he says softly. "That's my job, Tara. That's my purpose in life."

But my hand is already moving down. It's sliding along his hard stomach and under the sheets. When my fingertips arrive at his cock, it's already rock hard. I brush it lightly, gently sliding my fingernails along his shaft, and then I wrap my hand around it.

We're in the mountains, snowed into a cabin a million miles from civilization. There's nothing to distract us, so we can—

"Good morning!" a deep masculine voice shouts as the front door swings open. I leap up with a gasp as it slams into the wall, shaking the picture frames.

"Can you believe all of this snow?" another man says as the two of them burst into the cabin like they own the place. "It's got to be a new rec—"

The words disappear from his throat when he spots me sitting on the mattress beside Leo. I'm clutching the blankets over my bare chest and staring at him in horror.

"Guys!" Leo shouts. "Get out!"

"Who's *that?*" the older-looking one says as he points at

me. His eyes widen when he spots the mark on my neck. "Is that your mate?"

"Holy shit, it is," the younger-looking one says. "She's marked."

"Get the fuck out!" Leo roars even louder.

It's like they're both just realizing that Leo is here too. They look at him like they can't believe their eyes.

"You found your mate?" one of them asks.

"Why does she have a bandage on her nose?" the other one says as he turns to me. "Did he headbutt you during sex? Leo always was the clumsy brother."

"No, he didn't headbutt me," I say with a laugh. "It happened before I met him."

Leo is staring them down with a vicious look. "You have five seconds to leave or you're going to have a pissed-off grizzly bear to deal with and trust me, you don't want to deal with him around his mate."

"So, she is your mate," the younger one says, staring at me in disbelief. "Can we meet her?"

Leo grits his teeth. "*No.*"

"Come back in about ten minutes," I tell them with a smile. "We have to get dressed first."

"Okay," the older one says as they head back out. They're still staring at us in shock until the door is closed.

"Why did you do that?" Leo says as he puts his hand over his eyes and drops back down on the pillow.

"I want to meet your brothers," I tell him as I look around for my clothes. "Those are your brothers, right?"

"Yeah," he says with a heavy sigh. "Michael and Oliver."

"Let's get dressed and make them some breakfast!"

I jump up with excitement running through my veins. I

want to know everything about Leo and this is a whole side of him that I don't know anything about.

"We don't have to do this," Leo groans. "I can tell them to get lost."

"I think you tried that already," I say with a laugh as I quickly get dressed. "They didn't seem too responsive to the idea."

"I'll be more persuasive this time," he says as he cracks his big knuckles.

I chuckle. "We have all afternoon, evening, and night to be together," I tell him as I walk over, swinging my hips from side to side. "I think we can spare the morning."

I kiss him on the lips and he grabs me in his big arms. I let out a little scream as he pulls me onto his lap and kisses me so good I forget all about my morning breath. He doesn't seem to mind at all.

One thing quickly leads to another and that giant cock slides back inside me where it belongs. I'm straddling him and riding his big frame, gripping his shoulders as heavy moans rumble out of me.

It's a morning quickie, so it's not long before we're both cumming all over one another.

"Three minutes left," I whisper as I glance at the clock over the fireplace. "My new mates-in-law? Step-shifter-brothers? Whatever you want to call it, they'll be here soon."

I jump up, throw my clothes back on, and race into the kitchen to see what I can make with no power. I hope they like untoasted bread with peanut butter.

"I'll get the generator started," Leo says as he gets up with a groan and puts his pants on. "If we're going to do this, let's do it right."

Michael and Oliver join us and we all make a huge feast

together. Coffee, eggs, bacon, French toast, sausages, the works.

It's a ton of fun and we spend the day at the table, talking, laughing, and getting to know each other.

It already feels like home.

By mid-afternoon, I'm not ready for it to end, but I'm glad it does...

Leo kicks them both out and locks the door.

The ravenous look in his eyes when he turns around makes me shiver in anticipation.

I'm hoping there's more snow on the forecast as he approaches with a lustful gaze.

I don't want that door to open until spring.

Chapter Eleven

Tara

"This snow is amazing," I say as I let myself fall backward. I sink into it and start doing snow angels while Leo laughs.

The sun is out and the snow has finally stopped after a couple of days. It might be a new record. Poor Leo had to shovel out the front door so we could get out of his house there was so much snow.

Leo drops beside me and makes a much larger snow angel.

"What do you want to do today?" I ask, already knowing what his answer will be. We'll probably end up doing what we did the past few days, which was each other. In every room. In every position.

It's been an amazing couple of days.

"You know what I want to do," he says with a grin as he

looks at me. "But before all that, I think it's time to call your mom."

My stomach sinks as I look up at the bright blue sky.

I've been putting that off. I've been dreading it.

This place has been a perfect little oasis. Being stranded here with Leo has made me feel like the outside world no longer exists. Like it's just the two of us left on the planet.

I don't want that feeling to end. I don't want to pick up a phone and get sucked back into the real world where my mom is furious with me and people think I'm a huge bitch for ditching my groom at the altar.

I just want to stay here in this blissful place with Leo a little longer. I'm not ready to go back yet.

"They must be worried sick about you," he says. "I know I would be if you were driving in that storm and I hadn't heard from you."

I sigh. I know he's right.

But... I'm not ready to talk to my mother yet.

"I'll call my sister, Cynthia," I say.

"I'm sure she would appreciate that," Leo answers.

"Fine," I say as I sit up. "But I want something in return."

He grins as he looks at me. "You know I'll give you anything. I can't say no to you."

"Bring your grizzly bear out," I say with an excited smile. "I want to meet him again."

He huffs out a breath.

"Come on!" I say, clapping my hands. "I was so out of it the last time I saw him. Plus, I thought he was going to eat me so I was intolerably rude. I'd like to be friends with him."

He looks at me for a long moment and then smiles. "Alright," he says with a shrug of those big shoulders. "I'll let him out."

I'm smiling from ear to ear as he pulls off his light sweater and then starts taking off his pants.

"You're just going to get naked in the snow?" I ask with a laugh.

"Yeah," he says with a grin. "Otherwise my clothes are going to get shredded to pieces. Surprisingly, my full-grown male grizzly bear doesn't fit in my t-shirt and jeans."

I nod my head and grin at him. "That is surprising."

Even though we've been going at it like rabbits over the past few days, I still let out a little gasp when he pulls his boxer briefs down and I see his big long naked cock.

I keep my eyes locked on it until his huge body starts shaking as he phases into his bear. Everything swells up. His shoulders, his chest, his arms, his legs—they all expand lightning-fast. He groans in pain as his teeth lengthen into sharp white fangs. Long brown hair spurts from his skin and then with a tear, a full-grown grizzly bear explodes out of him.

"*Whoa,*" I whisper as he lands on his four paws so hard I feel the vibration through the ground.

I know it's Leo in there, but it's still shocking to see a massive animal like that in front of me.

He looks at me and I gulp.

"Hello," I say in a shaky voice. "Are we going to be friends?"

Those massive shoulders move like boulders as he walks over with his head hung low and with his hungry eyes locked on me.

Leo wouldn't have let him out if he posed any danger to me, would he? Would he??

The giant apex predator walks right up to me, sniffs my neck, and then presses the top of his head into my stomach.

I laugh as I sink my hands into his soft fur and scratch his skin.

The fear is gone. He's not going to hurt me. I can sense it just like I could sense that there was something different about Leo. This bear is my mate too. And he would do anything to protect me.

We play in the snow for a while and then Leo comes back out.

That worrying sensation in my stomach returns as we head inside and I realize it's time for that dreaded phone call.

Our little oasis bubble is about to be popped.

I take the phone to the fireplace, take a deep breath, and dial my sister.

"*Hold on,*" she whispers.

My heart is beating so hard as she hurries into another room.

"*What happened?*" she asks. "*Where are you?*"

I can't exactly tell her the truth. She thinks I've been hiding out in a hotel room by myself watching bad TV and eating room service non-stop. I don't know how she's going to react if she finds out I'm in love with a new man only a few days after skipping out on my wedding. Oh, and by the way, he's a bear shifter and I'm his mate.

"I'm safe," I say. Not exactly a lie, although it's not the full truth. "What happened after I left?"

"*Chaos,*" she says. "*I pulled David aside and told him first.*"

"How did he take it?"

"*He was relieved. Very relieved.*"

Oh, thank goodness for that. I'm happy we were on the same page about the whole thing, even though it does sting to find out that someone was relieved they didn't have to marry you.

"*He announced it to everyone,*" Cynthia goes on. "*Mom was not happy. She keeps complaining that she can't move to Argentina anymore.*"

"*Is that her?*" Oh shit. I can hear my mom in the background. "*Is that Tara?*"

"Don't put her on the phone," I say with my pulse racing. "Cynthia. Cynthia!"

"*Sorry,*" my sister says before handing the phone over.

I almost hang up, but I take a deep breath and power through.

"*Tara?*"

"Hi, Mom."

"*How could you do this to David?*" she says with contempt and disappointment in her voice. "*You two were in love!*"

I nearly laugh. In love? This lady's mind is already in Buenos Aires. She couldn't be farther from the truth.

"Mom, we were never in love! I think you saw what you wanted to see. Neither of us wanted to go through with this wedding. You and Marie practically shoved it down our throats."

"*I just wanted you to be happy. I was doing what's best for you.*"

"I think you were trying to get rid of me so you could move to Argentina."

She doesn't say anything.

"I'm moving out anyway."

"*You are? Where?*"

"I've learned a lot about myself in the past few days," I tell her as I glance at Leo. He's cooking lunch in the kitchen.

He glances back at me. This man always has a protective eye on me. I love it. "I met someone."

"*You did?*"

I want to tell her all about Leo and how he saved me and how he's a bear shifter and how strong our bond is, but she's going to think I've gone mad if I unload all of that onto her right now. I'll tell her eventually, but I'll take it slow.

"Thank you for the wedding, Mom," I say with a deep breath. "And thanks for trying to look out for me, but I'm fine now. I'll be okay from now on. You and Dad can live wherever you want. It's time you take care of yourselves for a change. Cynthia and I are all good."

She takes a few deep breaths. "*Are you happy?*"

I smile so wide my cheeks hurt. "I'm *very* happy."

We say our goodbyes and I hang up the phone and turn to my man. He's moving around the kitchen with his adorable gray apron on, already looking and feeling like home.

An intense appreciation of the world and everything in it settles into my body as I watch him.

"That sounds like it went well," Leo says as he spreads mayo on the toasted bread. "Would you like tomatoes on your sandwich?"

"Yes and yes," I say as I get up and walk over.

He raises an eyebrow as he watches me approach. "You're staying here with me, right?"

"If you'll have me."

"I'll have you," he growls as he swipes the counter with his arm, pushing the ingredients to the side to make some room on the granite. "I'll have you right fucking now."

I squeal as he picks me up and puts me on the counter.

That sexy lustful look in his eyes... *Holy fuck...* He looks like he wants to eat me for lunch.

My man is a *ravenous* one.
And that's just how I like it.

Epilogue

Leo

Thirteen Years Later...

I love snow days.

   We got about three feet of snow last night and it's still coming down. The roads haven't been cleared yet, so we're stranded here.

I'm so happy. This is exactly what I wanted—a day with my family.

The kids are thrilled because school is closed and the best part is, we lost electricity, so no Internet for today. All of the tablets, phones, computers, and video games are dead. I drained the batteries of all of them before I went to sleep last night.

I just wanted a fun family day with no distractions.

And that's exactly what we're having.

I smile as I watch my three kids in the snow. They're

pushing the middle ball for a snowman while I push around the enormous base. Tara is in charge of the head.

"I think that's big enough," Tara says with a laugh when she sees the ball I'm pushing around. It's up to my chest. "It's going to be August before that thing melts."

I love watching her in the winter. Her cheeks get all rosy and her green eyes sparkle. She has a colorful scarf wrapped around her neck and a cute little hat on her head. After all these years, I'm still obsessed with my mate.

"It might come in handy this summer," I say as I grin at her. "We can stick beer cans in it to keep them cold."

She laughs. "Now, you're thinking."

I smile as I watch her try to push the ball, but she keeps slipping. It's as big as she can get it.

"Need some help?" I ask with a grin as I walk over.

"Yes, please," she says with a sexy little smile. "Unless you want our snowman to look like he has a shrunken head."

The base I made is enormous, and our three kids are making a huge middle section too. All three of them are grizzly bear shifters, so they're incredibly strong.

I start rolling the head and making it bigger as Tara watches me with a loving look.

I still can't believe she's mine.

The thought of her nearly marrying another man always makes me sick. It turns out that David found the love of his life after Tara left him at the altar. He's happily married and they have a few kids too. Tara was happy to hear about that. I was just happy that he was out of the picture for good and she's all mine.

"Dad!" our oldest, Anthony, calls out. "Can you help us lift this on top of the base?"

"Sure," I call out. "Just roll it closer."

The three of them grunt and groan as they struggle to push it over.

"Oh!" Tara says as her green eyes light up. "I have an idea!"

I smile as I watch her run to the side of the house by the garden. Gratitude fills every inch of my body.

I adore that woman.

My inner grizzly grumbles in content as he watches her through my eyes. He's been so calm and happy this past decade with her in our lives. Nothing can upset him anymore. She has such a calming effect on both of us.

"What's that for?" I ask as she comes back with two flat rounded rocks.

She just grins at me. "You'll see."

My three kids help me lift the middle section onto the base and then since I'm the tallest, I grab the head and put it on top. It's a few feet taller than me.

Tara is right. This snowman is so big, it will be part of the family until school starts in August when it finally melts.

"Lift me up," Tara says with a grin.

She squeals in shock and delight when I grab her hips and lift her onto my shoulders.

"What are you doing, Mom?" Casey asks.

Tara sticks the flat rounded rocks into the top of the snowman's head and then reaches into her pocket for more. She places smaller rocks for the eyes, nose, and some twigs for whiskers.

When she's done, I step back to admire our masterpiece.

"It's a snow shifter," she says with a chuckle.

We all laugh as we see it. The flat rocks make perfect bear ears.

"I like it," our youngest Abby says with a big smile. "This is the best day ever."

The sun is out, the yard is full of snow, I have my three little cubs by my side, and my amazing mate on my shoulders. Pretty soon, we'll head in for some hot chocolate in front of the fireplace and play a board game while munching on snacks. The kids will go to sleep happy and tired, and then I'll have my sexy wife all to myself.

I have to agree with Abby.

This is the best day ever.

Every day with Tara is.

The End!

Continue with the Series:

Stranded With A Grumpy Cowboy
By Hope Ford

Stranded With An Alien Vampire
Michele Mills

More Shifters!

More complete shifter series are available now!

Get them on Amazon (in Kindle Unlimited)

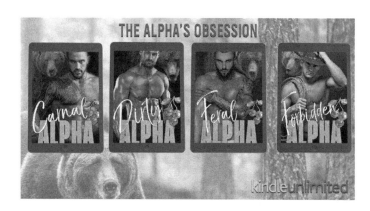

THE ALPHA'S OBSESSION

Carnal **ALPHA** · *Dirty* **ALPHA** · *Feral* **ALPHA** · *Forbidden* **ALPHA**

kindleunlimited

The Dixon Brothers

ALPHA *Possessed* · **ALPHA** *Consumed* · **ALPHA** *Dominated* · **ALPHA** *Unhinged*

kindleunlimited

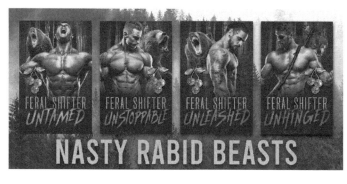

FERAL SHIFTER *UNTAMED* · FERAL SHIFTER *UNSTOPPABLE* · FERAL SHIFTER *UNLEASHED* · FERAL SHIFTER *UNHINGED*

NASTY RABID BEASTS

Follow Me...

Olivia T. Turner's complete list of books can be found at:

www.OliviaTTurner.com

amazon.com/author/oliviatturner

facebook.com/OliviaTTurnerAuthor

instagram.com/authoroliviatturner

goodreads.com/OliviaTTurner

amazon.com/author/oliviatturner

bookbub.com/authors/olivia-t-turner

Printed in Great Britain
by Amazon

36291735R00059